For Ezra, Roman, and Milo —D.W.
For Clara and Fanette —M.L.H.

Farrar Straus Giroux Books for Young Readers
An imprint of Macmillan Publishing Group, LLC
175 Fifth Avenue, New York, NY 10010

Text copyright © 2017 by David Weinstone
Pictures copyright © 2017 by Magali Le Huche
Color separations by Embassy Graphics
Printed in China by RR Donnelley Asia Printing Solutions Ltd.,
Dongguan City, Guangdong Province
Designed by Roberta Pressel
First edition, 2017
1 3 5 7 9 10 8 6 4 2

mackids.com

Library of Congress Cataloging-in-Publication Data

Names: Weinstone, David, author. | Le Huche, Magali, 1979– illustrator.
Title: All my friends are fast asleep / David Weinstone ; pictures by Magali
    Le Huche.
Description: First edition. | New York : Farrar Straus Giroux, 2017. |
    Summary: Unable to fall asleep, a little boy journeys from cave to sea to
    mountain peak, trying unsuccessfully to imitate the sleeping habits of his
    animal friends, until he finds the perfect place to lay his tired head.
Identifiers: LCCN 2016043679 | ISBN 9780374305352 (hardcover)
Subjects: | CYAC: Stories in rhyme. | Bedtime—Fiction. | Animals—Sleep
    behavior—Fiction. | Sleep—Fiction.
Classification: LCC PZ8.3.W42433 Al 2017 | DDC [E]—dc23
LC record available at https://lccn.loc.gov/2016043679

Our books may be purchased in bulk for promotional, educational, or business use.
Please contact your local bookseller or the Macmillan Corporate and Premium Sales Department
at (800) 221-7945 ext. 5442 or by e-mail at MacmillanSpecialMarkets@macmillan.com.

ALL MY
FRIENDS
ARE
FAST
ASLEEP

David Weinstone
Pictures by Magali Le Huche

FARRAR STRAUS GIROUX
New York

It's time for bed and overhead
the moon has risen high,
but I can't seem to fall asleep,
no matter how I try.

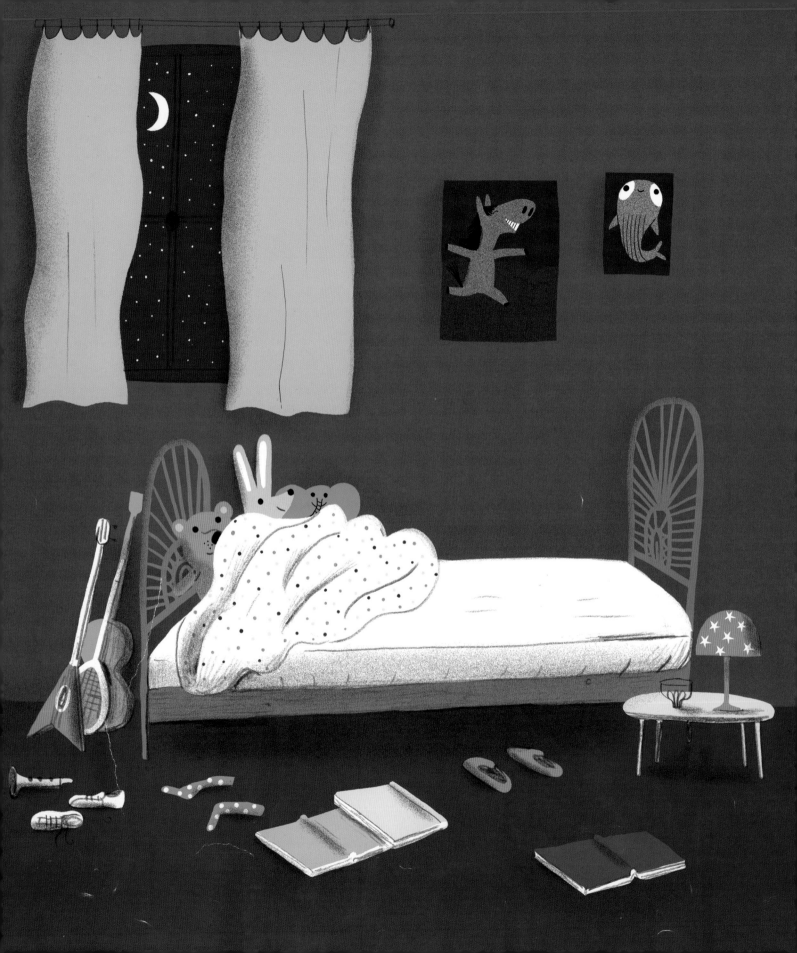

I toss and turn, I squiggle and squirm,
until I'm all worn out.
A different place to sleep I need—
of this I have no doubt!

So off I go to find a place
to lay my weary head.
Perhaps I'll find a friend or two
to help me up ahead.

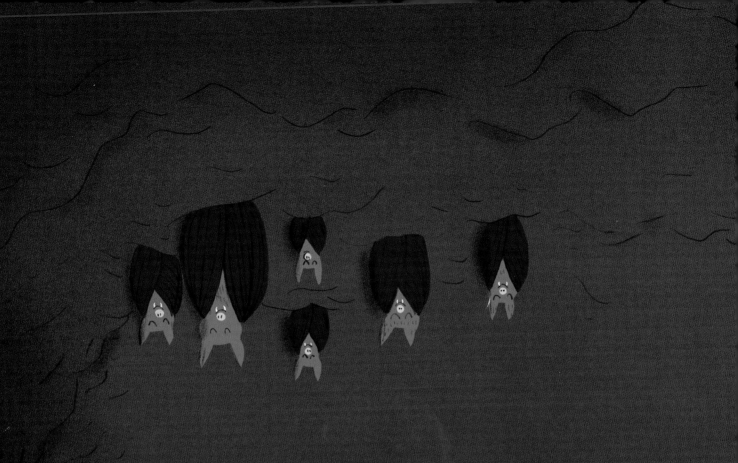

My friend the bat sleeps in a cave—
hanging by his feet.
A bat I'll be, I say to me,
but still I cannot sleep.

And horse, of course, sleeps standing up
among the cows and sheep.
A horse I'll be, I say to me,
but still I cannot sleep.

So on I go to find a place
to lay my weary head.
Perhaps I'll find a friend or two
to help me up ahead.

My friend the whale sleeps on the waves
that gently roll the sea.
A whale I'll be, I say to me,
but still I cannot sleep.

And little lark sleeps in a nest—
high up in a tree.
A lark I'll be, I say to me,
but still I cannot sleep.

The moon has risen higher and
the stars come out in bloom.
I hope I'll find a friend to help
me fall asleep—and soon!

My friend the mole sleeps in a hole
beneath a field of wheat.
A mole I'll be, I say to me,
but still I cannot sleep.

And woolly yak sleeps in the snow
atop a mountain peak.
A yak I'll be, I say to me,
but still I cannot sleep.

So on I go to find a place
to lay my weary head.
I know I'll find a friend or two
to help me up ahead.

My friend the frog sleeps on a log
beside a babbling creek.
A frog I'll be, I say to me,
but still I cannot sleep.

And silly seal sleeps on the rocks
along a sandy beach.
A seal I'll be, I say to me,
but still I cannot sleep.

So off I go, back to the place
where I had started from.
I've walked and walked and walked all night,
but now my journey's done.

All my friends are fast asleep,
from mountaintops to sea.
A boy I'll be, I say to me,
and shut my eyes to sleep.

ALL MY FRIENDS ARE FAST ASLEEP

Music and lyrics by David Weinstone

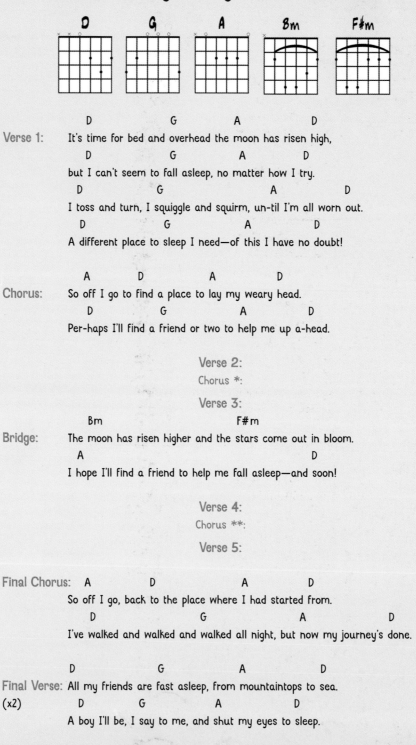

D   G   A   Bm   F#m

                D   G   A   D
Verse 1: It's time for bed and overhead the moon has risen high,
                D   G   A   D
       but I can't seem to fall asleep, no matter how I try.
                D   G   A   D
       I toss and turn, I squiggle and squirm, un-til I'm all worn out.
                D   G   A   D
       A different place to sleep I need—of this I have no doubt!

                A   D   A   D
Chorus: So off I go to find a place to lay my weary head.
                D   G   A   D
       Per-haps I'll find a friend or two to help me up a-head.

Verse 2:

Chorus *:

Verse 3:

                Bm   F#m
Bridge: The moon has risen higher and the stars come out in bloom.
                A   D
       I hope I'll find a friend to help me fall asleep—and soon!

Verse 4:

Chorus **:

Verse 5:

Final Chorus: A   D   A   D
       So off I go, back to the place where I had started from.
                D   G   A   D
       I've walked and walked and walked all night, but now my journey's done.

                D   G   A   D
Final Verse: All my friends are fast asleep, from mountaintops to sea.
(x2)   D   G   A   D
       A boy I'll be, I say to me, and shut my eyes to sleep.